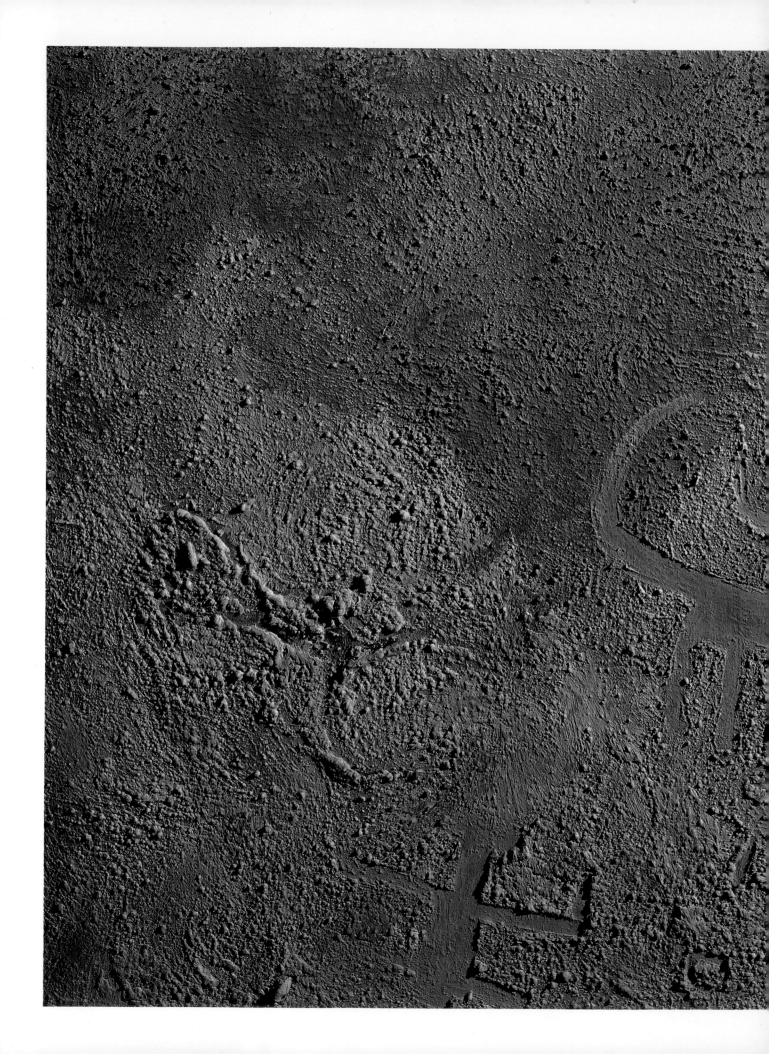

THE MUD FAMILY

BETSY JAMES

ILLUSTRATED BY PAUL MORIN

G. P. PUTNAM'S SONS · NEW YORK

The author thanks the many people who gave their time and attention to ensure the authenticity of this book, in particular Dr. Alfonso Ortiz of the University of New Mexico, Joe Dishta of the Zuni Tribal Council, and Zuni friends DruAnne and Phil Hughte.

The Anasazi, ancestors of the present-day Pueblo peoples, lived in the harsh, high deserts of the American Southwest. This book honors their skillful lives, celebrates the desert they adapted to so well, and praises what we too often take for granted: water.

Text copyright © 1994 by Betsy James. Illustrations copyright © 1994 by Paul Morin.
All rights reserved. This book, or parts thereof, may not be reproduced in any form without permission in writing from the publisher. G. P. Putnam's Sons, a division of The Putnam & Grosset Group, 200 Madison Avenue, New York, NY 10016.
G. P. Putnam's Sons, Reg. U.S. Pat. & Tm. Off.
Printed in Hong Kong by South China Printing Co. (1988) Ltd.
Text set in Gamma. Designed by Gunta Alexander.
Library of Congress Cataloging-in-Publication Data
James, Betsy. The mud family/by Betsy James; illustrated by Paul Morin.
p. cm. Summary: A drought threatens to force Sosi's family to move from their canyon, unless she can bring rain with her dancing. 1. Indians of North America — Southwest, New — Juvenile fiction.
[1. Indians of North America — Southwest, New — Fiction. 2. Rain and rainfall — Fiction.]
I. Morin, Paul, 1959– ill. II. Title. PZ7.J15357Mu 1994 [E] — dc20 92-43537 CIP AC
ISBN 0-399-22549-8 10 9 8 7 6 5 4 3 2 1 First Impression

For Abbey, Lisa, Larry, and Ken — B.J.

To John Wood, for planting the seed — P.M.

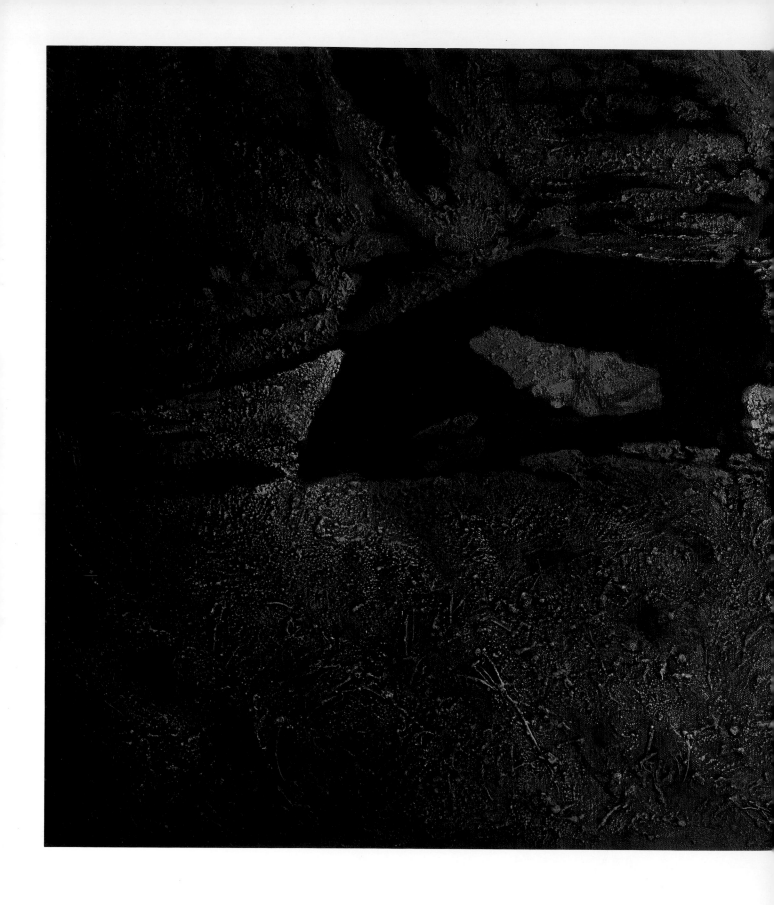

No rain falls.

In the canyon where we built our house the stream dries up into pools, the pools dry up into mud. A dragonfly darts overhead. Soon there will be no way to water the corn.

At our house, nobody laughs. They used to, but now the sky is hot and blue, the rain will not fall. My family is worried all the time. It makes them cross.

"Sosi!" they scold me. "Don't tease your sister!"

"Don't touch your father's loom!"

"Sosi, if you spill that, there's no more."

I spilled it, the whole bowlful, and I was hungry.

I don't want to live in that house anymore.

I go to the pool, and it is smaller every day. The dragonfly
dances. With wet red mud from the bank I make a new house
and a new family: father, mother, grandmother, two uncles, and
a girl bigger than any of them. No baby sister.

The hot sun dries them. I make the mud father say to his mud girl, "You are my lark, my lizard. I will weave robes for you and never scold."

I will live in my house forever.

Rain does not fall. The corn droops. At night my worried
father says, "Bring out the drum. We'll dance to ask for rain."
"I'll dance!" I say.

"You are too little to dance," my uncle says. "Go play with your mud dolls."

In the dark I run down to my mud family. I hear the drum for the rain dance, and I make the mud mother say to her mud girl, "You are my rabbit, my antelope. When you dance, the corn grows."

Nobody knows where I am. When my real mother calls me, I do not answer her for a long time.

Rain does not fall. The pool dries up. There is no water, not even in the jars. The corn is dying.

My father digs a hole where the pool was, but the water that rises in it is cloudy and stinking, red with clay.

I play with my mud house. I make the mud grandmother say to her mud girl, "You are my swallow, my little frog, and nobody but you can come under my feather cloak."

The dragonfly is gone.

My father says, "Tomorrow we'll be gone like the dragonfly. We'll leave this house and find a place near water, a place where corn will grow."

"No!" I shout. "I won't go!" I'll never leave my mud house, my mud girl. "I'll stay," I tell them.

My mother packs our baskets and our bowls. Her face is tired and sad. "Sosi, tomorrow you'll come with us. We are your family."

In my head I say, You are not!

My father rolls up his loom. My grandmother cries, wrapped in her cloak.

Next morning I wake early. Everyone is asleep. The sky is full of fading stars.

I see our traveling bundles packed and ready. I walk down to the dry pool, to my mud house.

"*You* dance for rain," I whisper to my mud girl. Under the pale sky she dances. "Rain, rain," I say. I drum with my feet on the dry dirt. "Rain for my family," I sing.

The stars have vanished. The dawn sun is hidden in a cloak of clouds. Wind rises, bending the grass.

The dry corn rustles.

One raindrop falls, then another, and suddenly it is raining, raining straight down out of the morning sky.

The air is sweet with wet stone. My father, my mother, my two uncles wake and stare.

Laughing and crying, they shout, "Rain! Rain!"
My grandmother wraps my sister in her cloak and shows
her how to touch the water falling from the sky.

I kiss my mud family. I put them inside their house.

"Thank you," I say. "Now we can all stay."

The rain falls hard. A thread of water fills the stream and spills into the pool. Up in the canyon I hear a sound like rushing thunder, louder than the rain.

My father calls, "Sosi, quick — jump to me!"
But, "My family!" I cry, and I run to my mud house.

My father sees me.

"Sosi!" he shouts. A red wall of water taller than I am is rolling down the canyon, frothing and boiling, tumbling logs and leaves.

Too late. It is gone, pouring away down the canyon as my
father snatches me and jumps up the bank, holding me high.
The new red river tumbles by, twisting like a snake's back.

I cry. "My family is drowned!"

My father holds me close. "We are your family," he says.

"The other one is free again. It is wet mud for growing corn, wet mud to make new dolls and to build houses."

"She brought the rain," I say. "My mud girl."

"*You* are my mud girl," my father says. "You are my dove, my dragonfly. You are Sosi, who brings rain to my heart. Come."

We paddle our hands in the red mud at the roots of the corn plants. The stream flows, the rain falls.

On the walls of stone behind our house we lay our handprints:

father, mother, grandmother, two uncles, me, and even my
baby sister.

We can stay. The corn is growing. We are a family.

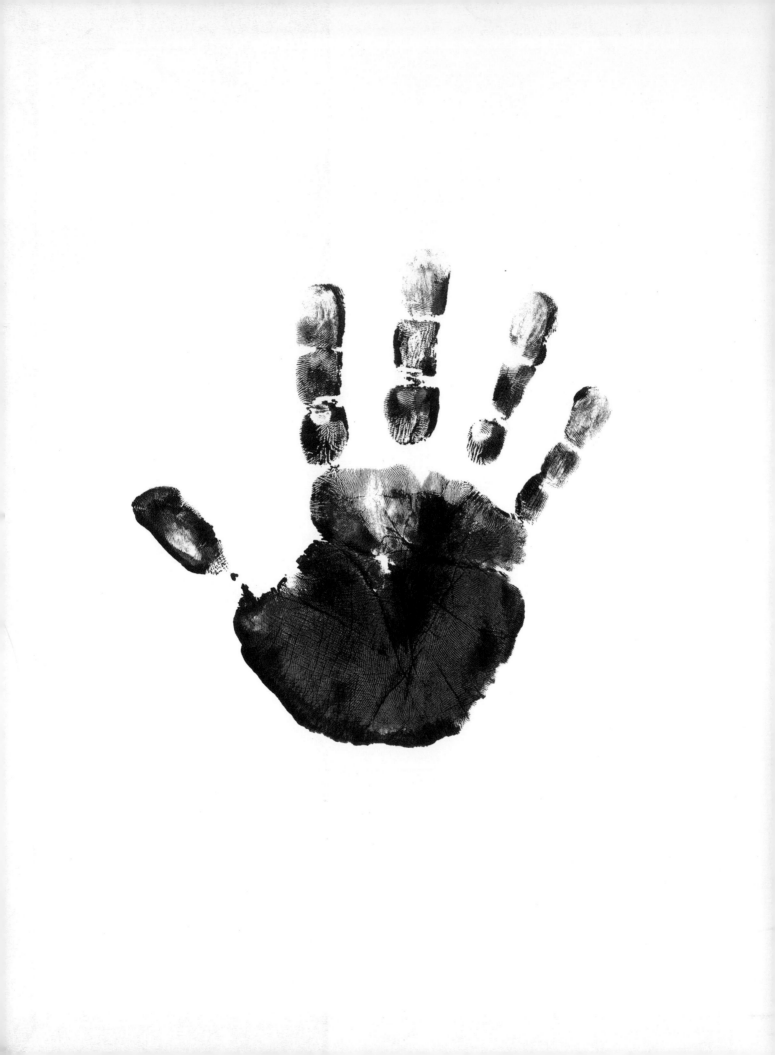